Also by Helen Claire Gould:

Floodtide

First published in the UK in 2018 by Helen Claire Gould
Books,

Peterborough, Cambridgeshire.

Cover Photographs:
Front cover: Callipso/Shutterstock.com;
Back cover: Vladimir Wrangel/Shutterstock.com

ISBN: 978-0-9930812-2-4

Printed and bound in England in 2015 by
4edge Limited, 22 Eldon Way Industrial Estate,
Hockley, Essex SS5 4AD

Dedicated to the memory of Graham Joyce.

Many thanks for your feedback and encouragement on this story, Graham.

The Stallion

Helen Claire Gould

IT WAS ON THE OUTSKIRTS OF THE SOUK that I first glimpsed it: pure white, a stallion, flared nostrils exhaling steam. Elemental, a figure out of the foundry of hell itself.

It trotted past the great trunks of the Caliban trees, weaving a pattern between them that paralleled their movements. Its eyes glinted red and wild in the sunlight, meeting mine with a knowing gleam and innate insolence. My pulse flared and the blood trembled in my veins, yet I couldn't look away. Despite my fear the horse's beauty caught at my heart.

The grey disappeared around the edge of the forest where the Calibans grew more thickly, and for several moments I stood staring after it.

*

I remember that morning well.

"Hurry up, Bashir – we'll be late!" my father had snapped. He'd moved so quickly that he was already waiting in the yard, muttering to himself, by the time I'd pulled my cloak around myself and hurried after him.

It was still dark outside. Stars were embedded in the sky like gems, winking down at us: provocative and mocking, unfulfilled promises in a galaxy of broken dreams.

"If the ships had come back when they said they would, we could've had everything irrigated properly by now," Father grumbled. "Even desert people have less chance of survival when they're just abandoned. Chance of a *better life* on Thargos IV – huh!"

"Maybe they *couldn't* come back. I wonder if other colony planets got what they needed?" I drew in a deep breath. "Maybe they'll come soon –"

"When the horses return?" he snorted.

1

Resentment stormed my heart. We'd had similar conversations before. *What can I do about the ships not coming back? I'm just a child,* I thought. *I can't make everything right for him. And why try to make me feel as bitter as* he *does?*

I've since realised that I wasn't old enough to bear his concerns as well as my own. But I was a good Muslim son; I'd never dare answer him back. So I swallowed my anger. As we brought the gra-mule into the yard the silence stretched between us.

Father was first to break it. "Ah, no use thinking of what might have been, boy! We're done for this time. The storm ruined everyone's crops."

Two nights before, sand had blasted over the fields – and not for the first time, but worse than any previous storm. Wind had roared around the house and defied any living thing to venture out into its fury.

Father was speaking again. "Ali doesn't know how he'll feed his family, let alone have crops left to sell." He sighed again. "I'll get some skins from the butchers today and cut some more sandal and purse pieces. You can help me sew them up while we're at market."

So – I'm not to go to school this *market day either,* I thought. I hated sewing the skins, though I knew the animals they came from were already dead. Though leather goods were my father's livelihood, I'd have saved every single creature.

But Father hadn't finished. "All we can do is hope the desert doesn't make us suffer for too long." He sighed. "Here, take the halter – you can always get the mule to behave."

Horses were rare and expensive. Camels hadn't adapted well to Thargos IV. Sheep and cattle were used for meat and milk, wool and hides. So three years before, Father had reluctantly bought a gra-mule, one of few indigenous types of animal which could be partly-domesticated. He'd regretted it ever since; I sometimes fancied, as it looked sideways at us, that it resented the arrival of us upstart humans. But it was better than carrying heavy leather goods to market on our backs.

Father loaded the panniers while I held the animal's halter, and talked and patted its neck the while. Its scales felt smooth; it was in the mood for work today. "Graah! Graah!" it brayed. It watched me with only an occasional sour glance at Father as he secured its loads. Then we set off along the track to the souk.

I drew in a lungful of crisp, dry, cool air as we walked; the dust had yet to rise to clog nostrils and throat. I smiled, but didn't let Father see. This was my route to school, and I always drew the same pleasure from the journey. All three continents of this world were dry desert for the most part, for they lay above and below the equator. But I loved the place. It was my home, where I was born.

Father had arrived from Earth with the first group of colonists. The second group had never arrived, nor the irrigation equipment or the ships. Twenty-six years he'd been here, with no hope of leaving. And I honestly believe that while I had nothing to compare my life to, he regretted coming here. *He's pained by its resemblance to the Earth,* I realised, *and permanently short of temper. He always said this land took everything he ever had.*

In the distance, dawn brightened the horizon's edge. Scrub, red dunes, and a few gra-mules and smaller animals were the desert's only population, with maybe a herd of horses if you believed old Sadiq's tales…

Ahead lay the forest: huge trees with scaled trunks towered over the track. Calibans, the first exploratory team had unkindly called them, for the strangeness of their appearance. The name had stuck. Squat and splay-branched, their foliage drooped in sparse clusters far above us. Every morning all the trees' limbs pointed west, towards the rising sun, while sundown saw them point east. During the day, massive boughs, which stretched high above our strung-out settlement, sometimes interwove in a slow-motion dance, and raised a wind to stir the sand. I'd watched them as a child, kneeling to pray on my mat in the yard.

A breeze stirred now. Insects buzzed in the scrubby underbrush that grew between the bare trunks. We trudged on, the gra-mule ambling between us. The Calibans' pendulous leaf-rods, which had surely elongated again these last few days, swayed as if to voluptuous rhythms unsensed by Father or me.

<Man is a mere insect,> their wind-dance whispered to me, <a late-comer to this our land. We have been here since the start of time. And we will *still* be here when awareness flees the universe.>

I was startled for a moment, then dismissed the ideas in my mind as mere fancy.

We emerged into the first of the forest clearings. I heard the babble of people – moving, working, talking. Behind me, the sun peeped over the dune-straddled horizon and gilded the outlines of leading branches and trunk-edges. I walked backwards a few paces to watch the light grow in the western sky. Then the gra-mule coughed – usually a sign of trouble. I stroked its neck. Ahead, the next patch of forest leered at us.

"Not far now," Father said.

I thought I heard movement in the scrublands at the wooded area's fringe. Before I could decide which direction it came from, we plunged between the Calibans again. Greater numbers of leaf-rods swung closer together here. I listened for the sound of water which came at this point, and was soon rewarded: an underground stream, no doubt, rushing to join the river that fed some of this land. We'd never found the spring, though we'd often looked. On the desert world of Thargos IV, water was a greater bounty than gold. The other side of the forest hosted most of the farmlands, being more fertile than the east where we lived. Date palms rubbed shoulders with other plants from Earth and local flora, and Calibans shaded the land for some kilometres.

The trees grew closer together here, but in the next clearing lay the souk. The monstrous trees grew between the stalls; their shadows kept the worst of the midday heat from the stalls and told traders when to return home. And where the trees grew there must be water to bring fruitfulness to this parched land. The builders of Adiba had found a place where they could live well, at least for a time.

Patches of sunlight burst between branches as they unwove. I shaded my eyes with my hand. It became clear to me that we *late-comers* received these benefits from the Calibans, yet gave nothing in return.

I dismissed the thought as we approached our pitch. Around us, women chattered and presided behind stalls while their husbands brought additional wares to pile high on the wooden constructions. Some of that wood had come from Caliban trees.

"Look sharp now!" Father said. "If you dawdle people will have spent up and won't have anything left to buy our goods!"

It should have been my mother helping him, or my older sisters. But the desert chills had claimed all of them many winters ago, one after the other. Father often said that if the ships had come, they might still have been alive.

"Help me get the stall ready. We're late enough as it is. And don't stick your lip out like that, Bashir – I know what you're thinking, and it isn't any use wishing for the past."

I was surprised. Father wasn't usually as perceptive as that; he was mostly wrapped up in his own thoughts. I wondered if he'd been smoking the stimulant which grew in a corner of the yard, as I knew he sometimes did. Then I remembered that my own senses seemed sharper this morning as well. With a shrug which dislodged the cloak from my shoulders I led the gra-mule alongside the stall. I was glad to feel air against my skin again; though dust and heat hung in the atmosphere.

"Hey, Muzzammil! Don't let the Superintendent catch you making Bashir help you again!" someone shouted.

5

My father scowled at the next stall and continued unloading. He laid my cloak to one side so it wouldn't be mixed up with skins or goods. In the distance, I thought I could hear hoofbeats. I ignored them, and the leap of hope and fear which came with them.

When Father had cleared the gra-mule's back, I led it to the grassy area at the other side of the souk where all pack animals were tethered. Here the occasional terrestrial camel snootily avoided rubbing shoulders with gra-mules, shaded by the Caliban forest. While they rested, a few horses nibbled real grass, grown from seed from Earth, and their riders went about their business in the bazaar. A movement caught my eye. Between the legs of a camel skittered a small desert-dweller; we called them desert hares. In truth, they were more like lizards than rodents.

I drew the gra-mule to a post sunk in the ground, hobbled it with the halter, and stood watching it. A blast of heat and light struck me as one of the nearby Calibans shifted. I fanned myself with my hands. The gra-mule gave me a long stare, then turned away to munch on tough brownish stalks, the nearest equivalent of grass on Thargos IV. It bore little resemblance to terrestrial grass; leafless, it had only stalks and roots.

On the way back to my father's stall I passed old Sadiq. His forehead and crooked nose bore several horseshoe-shaped imprints, and the keffiyeh which framed his face did nothing to cover the scars or opaque pupils. As usual, a crowd of children were gathered around him to hear his stories. Even adults at nearby stalls paid him attention between customers. I'd listened too, many times: to stories about the Landing, stories of desert creatures of old Earth that nobody really believed in any more, to a hundred other tales of echoes of the past, things none of us children could imagine. The most popular stories with us were those about this land.

I caught a snatch of the story: "I was a horse-handler, the best, while I still had my eyes. That's why I came here, to care for the horses we brought with us."

My footsteps slowed. It was a tale I'd never heard before.

"But the ship was damaged on arrival, and horses are sensitive animals. Of all the things they dislike about starships, being suddenly released from stasis after a trip is the worst. So as I led the first screaming animal from the stalls and down the ramp, the creature bucked and stood nigh upright. He was a great stallion with the purest white coat I'd ever seen – and I'd seen a lot of horseflesh! And his eyes were pale and without pigmentation, a manifestation of a mutated virus from the frontier planets. But as he glared at me they were red with fear and anger.

"My last sight was of his hooves striking for my face. Then the pain came, and I crouched on the ramp. My hands covered my broken face while his hoofbeats thundered into the distance, and a hundred horses streamed after him into the desert. I was lucky not to be trampled to death in the stampede." Sadiq sucked in a quivering breath.

For a moment I feared he wouldn't be able to continue speaking.

But after a convulsive swallow he continued. "Nearly all the horses escaped with that grey, so there are few in Adiba now, and most of the traders –" Here Sadiq waved a hand at the stalls around him, despite his inability to see them. "Well, don't your fathers use the lizards as pack-mules?"

"Yes, and much trouble they are, too," someone muttered nearby. Children giggled.

Sadiq waited till the chuckles subsided before speaking again. "And so we've learned to associate the return of the horses with the return of the ships..."

I remembered then that I was on an errand for my father. As Sadiq began a new tale, I wandered back to the stall. The sun rode higher in the sky and its heat drummed at my temples. But as I threaded between booths near the outskirts of the bazaar, where Calibans and bare red earth gave way to native grasses...that was where I saw the stallion.

7

And Sadiq's story came back to me. I let out a shuddering sigh, blinked moisture from my eyes, and hastened my steps.

Father had already laid everything out. On the stall, shaded by hides nailed to a wooden frame, lay great piles of tooled and plain leatherwork: the little bags for carrying the Qu'ran, belts, purses, sandals, shoes and boots, these last nearly tall enough to keep the fine quartz grains from sifting between the toes to chafe them. There were supple leathern cloaks and scabbards for the curved swords that some of the men still wore, relics of the old days on Earth.

"Where were you, boy?" Father growled.

"Tethering the mule." I injected innocence into my words. I wasn't ready to share my vision of the horse with him, nor would I have revealed my earlier fancy that the Calibans were trying to tell me something. *He'd laugh, or say I was daydreaming.*

"I've been asked by the teacher to find out if your son's here again, Muzzamil?"

We both turned. The Superintendent always rode a bay horse with a regretful air. I was near enough to smell leather polish and sweat. The mare gazed at me, flicking her black tail to dislodge grazing insects, and I realised for the first time that her expression echoed her rider's. "I do hope you're not encouraging Bashir to miss his schooling so he can help you on the stall again –"

"No, no, not at all!" Father lied.

The mare turned her reproachful gaze on him.

"I'm glad to hear it," said the Superintendent, and walked his mount away from the stall. He was a man of power, the source of order within our community, the possession of a horse his badge of office. I gazed after him for a moment, envying him the bay. And yet not, for she could in no way stand up to comparison with the magnificence of the white stallion, though I was almost sure I'd dreamed that creature after all.

8

"You'd best get to school, then, son," said my father. "Don't forget this." He took a pocket-sized copy of the Qu'ran from the leather bag around his neck, kissed it, and handed it to me. To protect it he'd bound the Qu'ran in fine skin he'd cured himself. I took it and kissed it. Then he handed me the bag from round his neck. I shortened the strap and slipped it over my neck, then slid the Holy Book back into it, so that it lay against my heart.

Beside me, Father spotted a potential customer and yelled, "Fine leathers!"

I turned to go.

Hooves pounded the earth as the white stallion thundered round the end of the stall. It stood before me for a moment and pondered the wares laid there. Then its eyes roved across the stall to Father, then to me. An unnatural hush fell on the souk. In the distance a child cried.

I dared not move.

The great horse's flanks expanded. Its wild spirit and nobility filled those eyes: red and slitted, they reflected the sun in the clearing. The marketplace rabble receded. For a moment there was only myself and the stallion in the bazaar, boy and horse juxtaposed, the wild and free against the chained. Then it drew itself in, and determination filled its eyes.

It moved closer.

It was huge. I stepped back involuntarily as I remembered how Sadiq had lost his sight. I held up my hands in a warding gesture; a pang tightened my stomach.

It shook its head. Its silky mane flew in several directions at once – though the air was still. Its breath was hot on my skin.

I turned and ran. The Holy Book bumped against my breast. I laid a hand against it to protect it. In between stalls and people I dodged. Round a fruit booth. Rich scents of peaches and dates mingled in my nostrils. My arm caught a basket. Melons thudded on the ground.

Hoofbeats clattered behind me.

I dared not check how close the horse was. I spun to my right and pushed between traders.

One of them shouted. No doubt he thought it a child's game. Ahead, people jumped back.

I wasn't sure if they sought to avoid me or the stallion.

The hoofbeats were louder now. Terror invaded me. To my right was a stall crammed with brasswares. I sensed sanctuary within the frame, twisted and dropped to the ground, wriggled between the planking and curled up, and hoped the stallion wouldn't see me in the gloom. Through a gap in the drapes I saw the stallholder's ankles.

He stood before his stall. "Only eighteen credits for this vase!"

"Too much at that!"

The stallion skidded to a halt that scuffed up a cloud of sand by the stall. His head swung from side to side. He still sought me.

I felt his presence. *Can he sense mine?* The idea panicked me.

There was a crash from behind as the stallion reared up and kicked at the booth.

I crept towards the light at the other end of the frame. *If I can escape without him noticing –*

But as I squirmed back into daylight the stallion awaited me. I backed away and dashed towards Father's stall. Out of the corner of my eye I saw the Superintendent ride up to a trader and shout something. The man nodded and turned away.

I hardly had time to think. At my back I felt a stall's planks, and smelled the reek of leather; I'd circled the bazaar. Someone screamed.

Father was on his knees. He wrung his hands before the great horse. His lips moved.

But I couldn't hear what he was saying. I turned to face the stallion. His breath on my skin was hotter than the sun. The sounds of the marketplace receded, replaced by a sense of isolation from the rest of humanity. The stallion stood regarding me with that same quizzical look of reproach that the bay had worn. The Superintendent dared not approach.

I knew I had to get away from this insane creature. Surely he intended to kill me, or at least maim me as he had Sadiq? I thought to climb one of the trees. *But what if it moves as I climb?*

But the top of our stall was sturdy enough – dead Caliban-wood was forever stilled. I scrambled upwards. From my vantage point I looked around. I remember the brass nails in the top of the stall, holding planks and skins together. The smell of leather and sweat hung raw and crude in the air, like distant battlesmoke. I couldn't see Father.

He must have fled.

The stallion nudged the planking.

I felt it shake and settle again. I clung to the frame.

The stallion reared and struck the stall with hooves that glistened in the sunlight. Leather tore. The lower planks split like matchwood.

My heart jerked. I clung to the centreframe, then pulled myself astride it. I crouched, unable to go anywhere. I was trapped. In the background a voice repeated the same phrases over and over, but I couldn't make sense of the words.

The carpet booth stood hard by our stall. It was just near enough to pull myself over. I wriggled along the centreframe. At the end I cast a look at the great white horse.

He stared back at me.

I gathered myself up. I grabbed for the next stall-top, as I tried to escape the fate this creature had decided for me. All the while I held his gaze.

My hands struck the centreframe and bounced off, numb. I discovered then that Caliban-wood was hard as iron, even cushioned with the skins. I lost my grip and slid down the shade. My world narrowed down to a sheet of red leather, to clawing for scale-barked wood with hands that didn't quite work, to listening between gasps for the hiss of breath and the sound of hooves.

But I heard other sounds: the creak of leather and swish of fabric as men moved, a clash of metal followed by a curse, arrows nocked to bows, swords slid from scabbards.

Understanding came. *They're going to kill the stallion.* Fear and sorrow overwhelmed me. His beauty had captured my soul, despite Sadiq's loss.

"Ready?"

That one word was clear – even against the background jabber of the souk.

Tssooosh! An arrow slit the air. It buried itself in the wood not an arm's length below me. The shock ran through the stall-frame.

I turned to face the Superintendent's men. Leather split under my weight. Appalled, I slid earthwards. The wooden edge of the stall caught under my arms, and the jolt numbed my shoulders and winded me. My legs dangled in the air. I realised the voice I heard was Father's as he prayed.

The white stallion shrieked a protest and thundered towards the archers.

I heard them scatter.

There were more hoofbeats. Teeth closed on my leg.

I knew fear and expected pain. Strangely, none came, though the stallion had gripped my leg in his mouth. I dared turn to look at him as he tugged at the limb. His eyes were white too, but hot as ever, fuelled by desperation. That made us equals, each in our own way.

The stallion released my leg. I felt his nose against me, exploring. He passed alongside, nudging me, and held my gaze with a look as purposeful as any man's.

Of a sudden I realised I'd misunderstood his intention all along. Weak with relief, I allowed myself to drop onto his back. I bent my head to his ear and whispered, "What *is* it that you want?"

I caught a glimpse of Father crouched near the ruin of our stall. My cloak was folded up in his arms. Nearby, the

Superintendent's men regrouped. There were shouts from them. "This way, Bashir!"

"Ride him over here!"

Now they plan to trap the stallion, I realised. I held up my hands, to which awareness was flowing back in painful pulses, to stop the archers from shooting. "It's all right!" I called. "Put down your bows and arrows. He means me no harm."

My father's voice was louder than the rest. "Bashir! Come here, son!" He ran towards me, but two of the Superintendent's men grabbed him. He struggled in their grip. "Curse you, man! I want my boy safe. Let me get to him!" He freed himself from one man with a punch.

But the other held on tight. "Don't be a fool, Muzzamil – that's a rogue horse there –"

The stallion drew in a lungful of hot air and whinnied a protest. He gave me no time to regain strength in my hands. We were away. I clung to his mane and lay low against his neck. Not even the Superintendent dared follow us.

We headed out into the desert, away from the Calibans. The sun bombarded us with heat and dust. The great horse thundered along beneath me. After a while his hooves no longer sounded like steps, just urgent drumbeats. I narrowed my eyes against the wind. The dunes blurred red around me. My hands had passed through the stages of numbness and pain and arrived at a place where only occasional hot needles stabbed them.

I gasped for water as we slowed. My eyes were full of grit. The sun had passed its zenith, so as blessed shadow fell on us, I squirmed upright in surprise and looked around. It hurt to move. I'd lain stiffly against the stallion for hours. Every muscle ached with the effort to stay on his back.

An overhanging cliff shaded us. The grey picked his way among boulders rounded by the passage of ancient waters. He'd run from dune to dune, and hadn't tired, though the sand had shifted and flowed under his hooves. We meandered along the gully.

My thirst increased in steps as I gulped air. In the distance I saw a mirage of Calibans. It occurred to me to wonder if the stallion also suffered in the dry gritty atmosphere. As we skirted another boulder, I realised that the Calibans were growing closer. *No mirage, then. There must be water there,* I thought, *but water locked up in the land, so that only the roots of those great trees can reach it. I shall die of thirst here in the desert, far from Father and my home.* Still the shade of the cliff-edge was welcome...I drifted into a few instants' sleep, then awoke with a jerk to find the stallion had halted before the great trees. He blew gently, as if unfatigued.

I stared upwards. The leading branches pointed towards the sun; the trailing branches followed. For once there seemed to be some significance in this.

As I watched, first the pendent leaf-rods trembled as if shivering in a stiff breeze, then the great limbs began to stir more quickly than I'd ever seen before, creating a wind which dusted my clothes with loose sand. Thoughts came to me.

<Know this, O little man-thing,> they said. <This creature of horsekind is our messenger to you of humankind, as you will be to all your folk. We have chosen you through him, for he has told us of the bond long-held between man and horse on your homeworld.>

"Chosen me? How?" I croaked. Was my mouth dry from terror, or simple thirst? "I don't understand this. We – we thought you were just trees." If that was an insult, I hadn't intended it as such.

The Calibans ignored it. <He chose you because of your affinity with animals of this land and your people's, and because your sire is as much a rogue creature as his was.>

So *this* stallion was not the one who had taken Sadiq's eyes. I allowed my stomach muscles to relax.

<Through us, you and he are joined; a necessary thing for your task.>

14

"What kind of a task?"

The boughs interwove again, and I realised that as I'd watched them from my prayer mat in the yard I'd unknowingly been privy to their communications. <You will rid this land of your kind. Since humans arrived we have fought to free our world of you. We wish only to exist here at peace with our surroundings and gradually take back the land for ourselves.>

"Take it back?"

<When the continents drifted north, our lives changed. Watercourses dried up. The sand came and swallowed springs. Many life forms died. We can seek what we need below ground, but we will not allow human usurpers to change our world to suit themselves.>

It was true, according to our teacher: humans had gradually reshaped Earth according to their needs, and the aim was to do the same with every colony established in space. "But why have you waited until now to try to stop us?"

<We were not ready to enter the next stage of our life-cycle.>

"But our farmers would irrigate the land – you could spread – "

<Not so! Your folk have introduced new, thirsty crops to feed hungry people. These will cover the land if we allow it, to *our* cost. You are a danger to our very existence. You cut us down for your own use. And if you stay here, water will be diverted away from us and we will be the last of our kind.> The boughs ceased their movement for a brief space, then resumed. <Yet we have done all we can, and must now rely on a human child and an equine, with whose kind we have made our only bargain.>

Bewilderment sifted in to stifle my thoughts. "What have you done already, then?" I asked, though I was fearful of the answer.

<We sent the dust storms, and we will do so again and again, until your kind are gone from our world.>

15

"You have that much power?" I thought of the times I'd watched them from my prayer mat, and knew it was so. "What must we do?"

<You will discover that when you arrive. Drink now, then sleep, child-man! You have much work ahead of you.>

The stallion stood still and I slipped from his back. I realised then how far from the ground I was while I rode. I stroked his neck and nose, as I would have with the gra-mule.

A bough rippled and flexed, pointing to a boulder at one side of the gully. At its base, a spring seeped out among the stones, in what must be permanent shade.

"Come, then, fellow messenger," I said, and led the horse to the spring. I cupped my hands and drank deeply as he took a draught. "So it was your *sire* who blinded Sadiq, and not you? I'm glad, and I'm sorry I misunderstood your intention. I was so afraid. You're such a big horse – the biggest I've ever seen! I believe I should name you Akbar, which means 'greater' in my language."

He stopped quaffing and turned to look at me, but the fierce light was gone from his eyes; they were almost as white as his coat.

"I hope that means you approve," I murmured.

Next I washed myself in the manner of our faith. It was the time of day for prayer; and besides, I was disturbed, and knew that in my place Father would have sought comfort from reading the Qu'ran. I took the Holy Book out of its bag at my breast and kissed it. I faced the west, where Earth and the holy city of Makkah lay, knelt beside the boulder and turned the pages. But the sun was so bright it drew the meaning from the characters, and I could hardly see them.

<What is this?>

"Our Holy Book. It tells us how we should live our lives, and gives us guidance when we need it."

<What is your present difficulty?>

I thought before I spoke. But it was clear that I could only tell truth, for the Calibans would know what was in my

16

heart before I spoke it. "What you are asking of me will mean I must betray my people."

There was a long silence, punctuated by much branch-weaving, before the answer came. <We understand. You should rest now. Wisdom will arrive in due course.>

I shook my head and found my favourite prayer. Only when I'd finished chanting it aloud did I curl up against the stone. The sun warmed my back and my hand pressed the Holy Book against my heart. Akbar wandered among the Calibans; but I knew he'd come to no harm with them, and feared no abandonment. My eyes closed and I drowsed.

As I slept I dreamed of that furious chase through the souk again. But this time only the stallion's hoofbeats and my gasps for breath broke the silence.

My father had fled.

Between the stalls I dashed. Akbar was always at my heels. At the finish, with no more breath to run, his flanks heaved with the effort of pursuit. I grabbed a curved iron sword from Father's stall and turned to face him. He was taller than I'd imagined – almost as tall as a Caliban.

I knew with piercing certainty now that one of us would be destroyed. I felt crushed by sadness. He was so beautiful. I didn't want him to die, even to save myself. Yet I sensed it must be done.

I thrust upwards with all my strength. I don't know how the scimitar even reached him, but the stallion's belly ripped. Then I threw the sword aside as his sticky blood drenched me. Its metallic stink soaked into my clothes and skin, bringing with it the essence of the stallion himself. Hot steaming breath invaded the air with the violence of the foundry, shuddering as Akbar's life leached away in great broken gasps.

I curled myself up and rolled, protecting my head with my arms.

My sight performed a somersault. I stood over him, taller than any man had a right to be. I stared down at the thing on the ground. Crimson froth bubbled from the wound. It mingled with red sand and soaked into the thirsty land.

Thoughts came to me. *He was a creature of dreams. He was every dream that ever lived in any man's soul. And now those dreams are dead, all gone.*

And I reared up and threw back my head. I shook it so the breeze lifted my mane. I pawed at the wound to close it. But it was impossible: 1 no longer had hands, just swift, sure hooves and a message in my heart. So I cantered away westwards towards a rising orange sun, as a little moisture stung my eyes.

When I awoke I felt guilty and much disturbed. But my fatigue was gone, along with all trace of thirst and hunger. Akbar stood beside me as if waiting for me to wake. After that dream, looking him in the eye was the hardest thing I'd ever done; but he let me mount him and carried me towards the Calibans again. They were at peace, but as we approached their limbs threshed about, interwove in a pattern, separated, and interwove again. I realised there was now no question in my mind that I would accept their task; otherwise I'd betray my people all the more. There was no doubt that the Calibans were determined to protect their world, however they must.

<There is much to be done, bearer of good news.>

So they knew the meaning of my name. I hesitated, thinking on that. At last I said, "It seems you know much more about us than we know about you."

<You know all that is needful for now. Do not delay.>

I wanted to protest that I must know exactly what they required, but Akbar stepped towards the desert. To the east, the sun sank in the sky and stained the desert redder than ever in the dying of the day.

As night fell, I thought of Father, alone in the house where I'd been born and my mother and two sisters had died. I imagined him as he and the carpet-seller despaired over the ruins of their stalls, and then as he struggled home with the gramule. For a moment I saw him turn the pages of the Qu'ran, blind with emotion, and I wondered if he thought of me. Then I whipped up my own sandstorm to smother the vision, afraid to see his face. When the grains swirled away into the nothingness they'd come from I remembered the dream again, and how Akbar had shown me no fear, even though he knew he would die. Guilt seized me. My limbs trembled. I buried my face in his mane.

Akbar breathed in and picked up speed. The wind swept his mane into my face. I knew it was more that he carried me than that I rode him. I pulled my shirt closer around me and wished for my heavy leathern cloak. Chill air rushed against my skin like a thousand swords. One by one stars pricked the night sky above us, silent lanterns for our passage. The dunes were quiet; though I sensed the curiosity of desert creatures at times. A little dew came, and froze where it fell.

The headlong charge across the desert continued all night. When the ruddy blaze of sunlight licked at the western skyline I could swear the veins were frozen in my hands. Little by little the sun edged upwards over the dunes. Akbar never slowed his pace. As the sun climbed the sky my fingers unfroze on his mane. My skin was sore from the sand-scouring it had received.

Ahead a barchan dunefield reared out of the sand like the curves of a strange, regular calligraphy embossed on the land. One dune was larger than the rest and sloped south-eastwards, the opposite of the others. Akbar's furious run slowed as we breasted its crest. When he walked to a stop I slipped to the ground, and we stood and looked down into the dunefield.

Atop the incline lay a huge shape, part-exposed in the lee side of the monster dune that gave the lie to the wind direction. Curved strips of bright metal gleamed under the orange sunrise as they protruded aslant from the dune. I'd seen holos; it could only be a ship: one dome atop another; a third capped them.

So it had arrived at last, and some disaster had overtaken it. Judging by the dune's direction I had a very good idea of what had happened.

And then, from between the barchans, the horses streamed, one after another. There were so many, all sizes, all colours, all ages, each different. I thought it was the most beautiful sight I'd ever seen, after Akbar; like his first appearance, this will always remain etched on my mind and heart.

Akbar whinnied and stared at me. For a moment his eyes blazed like lamps, reflecting the colour of the desert. I stretched stiff muscles. The realisation came that he was as much at one with the land as the Calibans. I wondered what their bargain could have been.

But then he tossed his head to tell me to remount, so I vaulted up again. My fingers clenched in his mane, though it was getting easier all the time to stay on him, and I could sit upright as I rode now.

Akbar turned and cantered back downslope. He rounded the dune and slowed, facing the herd, before turning towards the ship.

A hatch swung open in its side. A man emerged and jumped down.

Two others followed him with spades. They stood talking for a few moments, and gestured at the horses, then at the ship, and once at me. The two with spades went to grub at the side of the ship. I ignored them.

The first man walked towards me. I watched him approach. Close up, I saw his skin was paler than mine, his eyes under narrowed lids the pallid green of Caliban leaf-rods.

He stared at me with a wary expression on his face. "I am Jean Capard." His Arabic was accented with an unidentifiable twang; my fellow colonists were all I'd ever known. "Are you from the settlement?"

"Yes. Have you brought the supplies and parts?"

He dipped his head. "We wondered if anyone was left alive here – after the war with the Lutai colony we sent one expedition after another, but every time ships tried to land, a sandstorm whipped up and we had to abort landing procedures.

We barely made it in three days ago, but got blown off-course in a storm and had to land here. The sand buried the ship." He gestured towards it.

"So I see," I said. "We thought Earth had forgotten all about us – our communications gear was among equipment destroyed during the landing."

"They told us that before we set off."

"Father says ships make a lot of noise, but nobody even heard this one arrive –"

"I am not surprised – that sandstorm was truly violent. Anyone with any sense would have stayed indoors!" Capard waved his hand at the ship again. "We have been trapped here since then. The exhaust nozzles are buried. We have tried to keep them free of sand, but it is hopeless." He paused, then pointed. "What are all these horses doing here?"

"They're here to help you."

Akbar moved under me; and the sting of sand grains against my hand told me the Calibans wanted to communicate with me.

"Get in the ship. Quickly!" I told him. "Another sandstorm's coming."

Capard shaded his eyes with one hand. "Where is the Superintendent of the colony?"

"You're many kilometres from Adiba," I said. "I'm all you have to deal with here."

"But you are only a boy!"

"I'm the messenger of the Calibans," I said. "And they would speak with me now."

"I do not believe you. The *Calibans* are just trees –"

"They're sentient trees. Look!" I pointed to the ship. "They did this. You do want the nozzles freed, don't you? I'll try to help – but I doubt you'll be allowed to land anything."

He cast a look of surprise and disbelief at me. He was still inclined to resist, though to give him credit, his hand never strayed to the holstered weapon at his hip.

I looked back at him. "Return to the ship!" I repeated.

21

He stood before me, frowning, his mouth a straight line.

The sand rose under the wind's goad. It funnelled up around Capard, Akbar and myself. Fear grew on Capard's face, in the greyish tinge of his skin and the widening of his eyes. But the sand never came near enough to do any real damage, and the Calibans' message was clear enough to me.

<Now we must undo the binding we put on this ship, so that your people may leave in peace before they destroy us.> The Calibans' desperation was as real as my father's back in the souk. <Ask this one for ropes. The horses will help. They will listen to you and the one you call Akbar.> The funnel of wind and sand subsided as the grains settled on the ground in a new pattern of ripples. The tension flowed from Capard's shoulders.

"How do you know what the Calibans want?" he asked.

"I hear their – voices – in my head."

"What do they say?"

I explained the Calibans' plan.

"We have earth-moving equipment intended for the colony that might help. The tractors would need constructing before use – but we could manhandle the hoppers and attach them to the horses with ropes. They would be perfect for shifting sand. But I do not understand why the horses should help the Calibans."

"I think they can stay here if they help them. And they have no wish to experience the fear and stress of another journey. Now hurry, find those hoppers!"

But Capard's persistence had set me thinking too. I watched him jog back to the ship with questions buzzing in my mind. "Why are the horses allowed to stay?" I demanded. "There must be some benefit to you."

Wind gusted and sand rose. <They disturb nothing here.> There was an evasive quality to the ideas in my mind. <We have no quarrel with them.>

I wasn't done questioning. "Why not just kill all of us?" *It's obviously within their power.*

22

<At the start of our fight against you, the equines came to us and asked us *not* to kill you, by virtue of the long and mainly mutually-beneficial association between them and humans. Our agreement is our word. Now, messenger, protect yourself. We have a task.>

Plumes of sand rose off the ship to form clouds. I glanced through slitted lids as the horses stood with eyes closed and backs to the wind to protect themselves from it. I dismounted and clutched the Holy Book against me for comfort, hid my face against Akbar's coat, and pulled my robe up to cover my face so I could breathe.

When the wind had eased, I dared look. The strange dune had lost its smooth outline and much of its bulk. Sand formed smaller dunes at its foot as the ship emerged from its prison. But the exhaust nozzles around the ship's lower edge were still half-buried, perhaps because the Calibans knew the blown sand could further damage them. *How can something so huge and impressive be so helpless before a force of nature?* I wondered. I mounted Akbar and trotted him over to the hatch.

As I reached it, it reopened. Capard and three crewmen manoeuvred the hoppers down, ropes slung over their shoulders. I gestured to bring the horses to me; they stood, patient, as I divided them into teams and we secured the first hopper on the nearest four horses. I moved among the herd, and tied on the hoppers.

They accepted their burdens without protest.

<This is an improvement on just ropes,> the Calibans approved. <The 'hoppers' will remove more sand, more quickly.>

They can't wait for the rest of us to leave. What's the hurry? But I had to set aside my suspicions to complete the work in hand.

The horses worked in teams, directed by the Calibans through Akbar and myself. I set one team to help shift the mound of sand on top of the ship, while another three groups hauled their hoppers to the sides and "back" of the ship – at least, it was opposite the hatch Capard and his men had used. By the time the teams were in position and ready to start, the sun had ascended in the sky.

The hatch opened and two men emerged with brooms. The sand was loose after being blown around. The men came and swept it off the top of the ship into the first team's hopper. The horses floundered on the sand as they dragged the hopper away. The men moved on to the next hopper.

It was crucial that the air intakes didn't become covered again once freed. I led the first team, with their cargo of sand, into the valley between the dune where the ship lay and its nearest neighbour. There they deposited the sand, helped by myself and another two crewmen.

The brooms helped expose more and more of the ship's uppermost surface, and soon I had to bring the horses back onto the sand to avoid damaging it irreparably. There were enough horses that the teams could be changed and rested regularly. All worked with determination and concentration, and all accepted the weight of the hoppers without question.

Soon the uppermost layer of the ship's hull was clear of sand. The sun blazed overhead, and only the crewmen still stood on the ship's hull, brooms poised to sweep the remaining sand off the next layer. I could smell their sweat.

Sand slumped from the middle dome to the lowest, where it formed a layer about a metre thick. Under the men's brooms it surged down into the waiting hoppers.

Although some piles of sand still remained, the whole rim of the ship gleamed under the sunlight. But as we worked the quality of that light changed and aged the day. My stomach growled with hunger, and I thought the horses' patience with their task had faded.

<We understand that you need sustenance, as do our friends the horses,> the Calibans agreed. <We shall finish this, messenger.>

At a gesture from me, the horses backed off. I led them away from the sting of sand grains, and within minutes the bulk

24

of the remaining sand had lifted under the Calibans' breeze. Capard's men and I released the horses from the hoppers. I took them aside to give them water indicated to me by the Calibans.

"The exhaust nozzles are almost clear," one of the men reported. "We can blow them now, and clear the last of the sand."

The ship quivered into life. It reminded me of one of Sadiq's ancient desert creatures. The engines' whine became a howl. Sand spurted in all directions from the eight exhaust nozzles. Soon the ship reflected the glare from the early afternoon sun.

"The ship was buried in twenty minutes," Capard told me, when we'd released all the horses. "It has taken all morning to clear it ready for take-off!" And to my surprise he offered me food. "You worked hard as well."

"So did your men."

<You should accept the food,> the Calibans advised. <We can only give you water.>

After that brief meal of strong coffee and bread I stood up. "The Calibans want you to go to Adiba," I told Capard. "I'll meet you in the souk."

This time he didn't doubt me, and with a nod, strode back to the hatch.

Though my confidence as a rider had grown, the trip back was another mad surge across the desert. Night crept in and stole away again before we came back to the stand of Calibans that marked Adiba. The ship's domes gleamed in the desert nearby. The people were clustered around Capard and his companions and the Superintendent when I arrived.

"Capard here has told me what happened out in the desert," the Superintendent said. "Is it right that the Calibans won't let him land the supplies and irrigation equipment?"

"It is. They fear losing access to groundwater. And they're angry about being cut down for firewood and building."

"But this is our home now – the more so for your generation."

I nodded.

"And without the supplies we'll all die. We can't save the crops this time."

Capard looked thoughtful. "You truly can communicate with these tree-things?"

"Yes. I'm their messenger."

"Then tell them this – that there is plenty of water for all in the oceans, although it is salty. We could bring desalination equipment from Earth." His face was open; truth rang in his words. "They would need have no fear of losing their water source, yet the colony could still irrigate the land, and they would also benefit from that."

I wish I'd known before, I thought. *I could have explained all this to the Calibans.* So I hastened to make good the delay.

Scaled branches far above intertwined in a stately dance, then separated. <Is this true?>

"I can detect no lie in his words," I answered them.

"Then why can you not all stay here?" Capard demanded. His light green eyes flitted from the Superintendent's face to mine. "Can the Calibans make some arrangement with you? Could the land the humans use for crops be limited and pre-agreed?"

<We have a solution. If you can take these hungry people away with you now, so that they may be fed, and bring the equipment here to desalinate the oceans, then they may return. But we must also no longer be another crop for you to harvest for fuel and building materials. If you lie, they may not return.>

I relayed the Calibans' suggestion.

"I am no liar!" said Capard. He turned to the Superintendent. "Will you organise the evacuation?"

The Superintendent nodded.

"We will need to leave our cargo here to make room for all of you, and we have no facilities for the animals," Capard continued.

<If your people are to return,> the Calibans murmured, <we shall have further need of your services, messenger. And the creatures left behind will need your care. Stay.>

I felt a hand at my arm. My father had pushed his way to the front of the crowd. In his hands he held my cloak. "Here you are, son," he said. There was no need for further words. *He knew I'd stay,* I thought. I allowed him to embrace me. There was a tension in his arms against my back. Then he released me and climbed aboard after Capard. He didn't look back, though I watched him. I thought it unlikely that he'd return with the others.

Preparations took up the rest of the day. The ship's cargo was unloaded and stored in some houses. Then, one by one, the faces I'd known all my life disappeared, swallowed up by the ship. Sadiq went last, headdress swinging around his face as the Superintendent led him up the steps. The bay mare he entrusted to me.

In the forest, Calibans threshed as the ship lifted, moving without volition for once. I stood pressing the Holy Book against my heart. The cloak around my shoulders echoed the trees' wind-dance.

The ship grew smaller and smaller, then disappeared.

Then I remembered the gra-mule at the house. Akbar nudged me with his nose. His eyes shone once more. I climbed onto his back and he trotted off through the trees, the mare following. The oasis was silent, but soon I could hear water. Akbar's steps slowed as the sound grew louder.

"Father and I never could find this spring," I told him as I dismounted.

Akbar just snorted, and swung his head. Before us, water welled out of stones near the base of a Caliban. I dipped cupped hands into its chill, felt the shock run up my arms, into the nerves in my armpits. I drank deeply. Akbar and the mare likewise guzzled thirstily.

"Well, at least there'll be water for us."

<Yes, messenger. You have served us well.> Above, the Caliban boughs danced again. <You will not thirst, or starve – we can show you where the land is fertile.>

I smiled as I stroked the horses' necks. "Come on, Akbar, just what was that bargain?"

For a moment I thought it was raining, though I'd only seen rain twice a year. Then I realised there was no moisture; Caliban leaf-rods carpeted the ground in a green-brown layer. Akbar stepped forwards and trod on them, an intent expression in his eyes. Soon the mare joined in.

"You aren't really telling me these were seeds all the time?"

Akbar swung his head to look at me. The knowing gleam made his eyes luminous in the dark.

<We would not allow our seed to fall until the horse-folk could do what we asked of them without interference from humankind, and without *their* assistance there would be no new generation of what your kind call Calibans. In the past there was another bargain, but the Dwervoo needed more water to survive, and died out as these lands moved into arid latitudes, though we were able to adapt by sending our roots down deep into a buried water source. Now that we need not fear being cut down our numbers will increase again.>

"Why couldn't the gra-mules spread your seeds?" I asked.

<Their claws haven't the power of a horse's hooves – our seeds are tough. Now make haste, messenger, for creatures of both this land and Earth await your care.>

I remounted and the horses cantered through the forest towards my father's house.

"Graah! Graah!" brayed the gra-mule as we approached.

Now I understand Thargos IV. Akbar and his equine companions are its inheritors, its true colonists, at least until my folk return. They live at peace with the Calibans, a balancing of the scales of nature. They are free, and willingly give their aid to the great trees. A little forest, just waist-high on me after five years, has established itself in the desert near Adiba.

I, too, have grown in that time. Since the day the colonists left, I have learned much from my discussions with the Calibans. I tend the horses, the sheep, the camels and cattle left behind, even the gra-mules. I grow my own food and am fed and provided with crisp-flavoured clear water, and never want for shelter.

And the desert is mine to wander at will, along with my faithful companion, Akbar. We share a bond, as the Calibans said. I believe I have learned Akbar's freedom of spirit in journeying with him. He carries me as willingly as ever; and I'd swear he understands me as my father never did. Him I know I shall never see again; but I am content with this life, at least until my own people return. Then I shall become the messenger of the Calibans again.

Our ancestors on Earth who once wandered among the dunes and stars of Arabia were free of all but their faith, as I am. And only a man who is truly free could live here on Thargos IV.

In time, I will become that man.

The Stallion is also available from Amazon as a Kindle e-book.

For further information about the universe of *The Stallion* and *Floodtide*, including starmaps, a timeline, and other forthcoming publications by this author, visit: www.Zarduth.com.

Look out for Helen Claire Gould's next novel, *The Zarduth Imperative: Discovery.*

ABOUT THE AUTHOR

Helen Claire Gould has been writing since her teens, having read her first two Science Fiction novels at the age of nine. At the Peterborough SF Club, where she met her husband, she contributed to the club fanzine *A Change of Zinery*. After suffering some miscarriages in 1992 she began writing for therapeutic reasons, joining Orbiters (SF postal writing workshops) and setting up the Peterborough Science Fiction Writers' Group. She edited two small press collections of short fiction, *Shadows on a Broken Wall* and *Mother Milk, Father Flywheel*, organised a weekend workshop on writing for comics, and had book reviews published in the BSFA review magazine, *Vector*.

Returning to full-time education in 1995, Helen graduated in Geology and Planetary science in 2000, teaching Geology and Creative Writing evening classes, and editing further collections of short fiction by her Creative Writing students. In 2013 she organised and ran a series of writers' workshops for the Peterborough Arts Festival.

Floodtide was Helen's first published novel, and was set in her own fictional universe. *The Stallion* is an ecological fantasy loosely based in that universe.